From the movie

Disney

FROZEN

EGMONT
We bring stories to life

First published in Great Britain in 2015
by Egmont UK Limited,
The Yellow Building, 1 Nicholas Road, London, W11 4AN

© 2015 Disney Enterprises, Inc.

Written by Mandy Archer. Designed by Diana Hill.

ISBN 978 1 4052 7795 2
60298/2
Printed in Italy

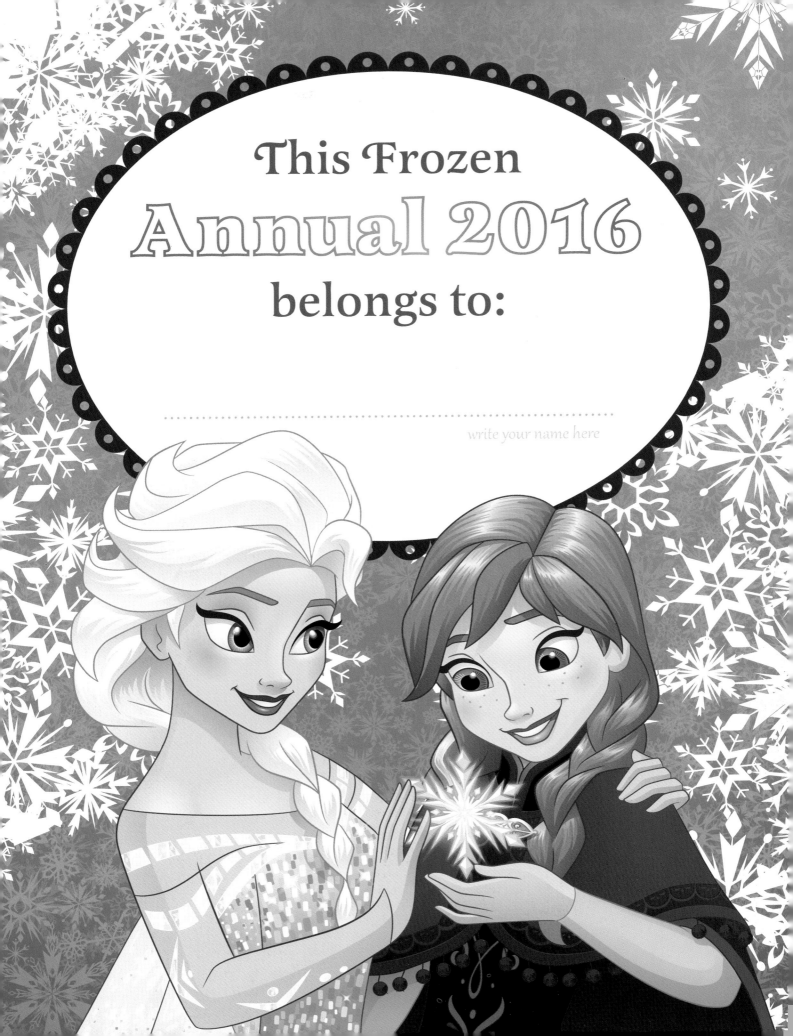

This Frozen
Annual 2016
belongs to:

....

write your name here

Contents

Frozen Fever

Step into Arendelle

Welcome to the Kingdom of Arendelle, an amazing land of mountains, forests and waterfalls. At its very heart is the royal castle, home to Princess Anna and Queen Elsa.

Peep into the castle throne room. What can you see?

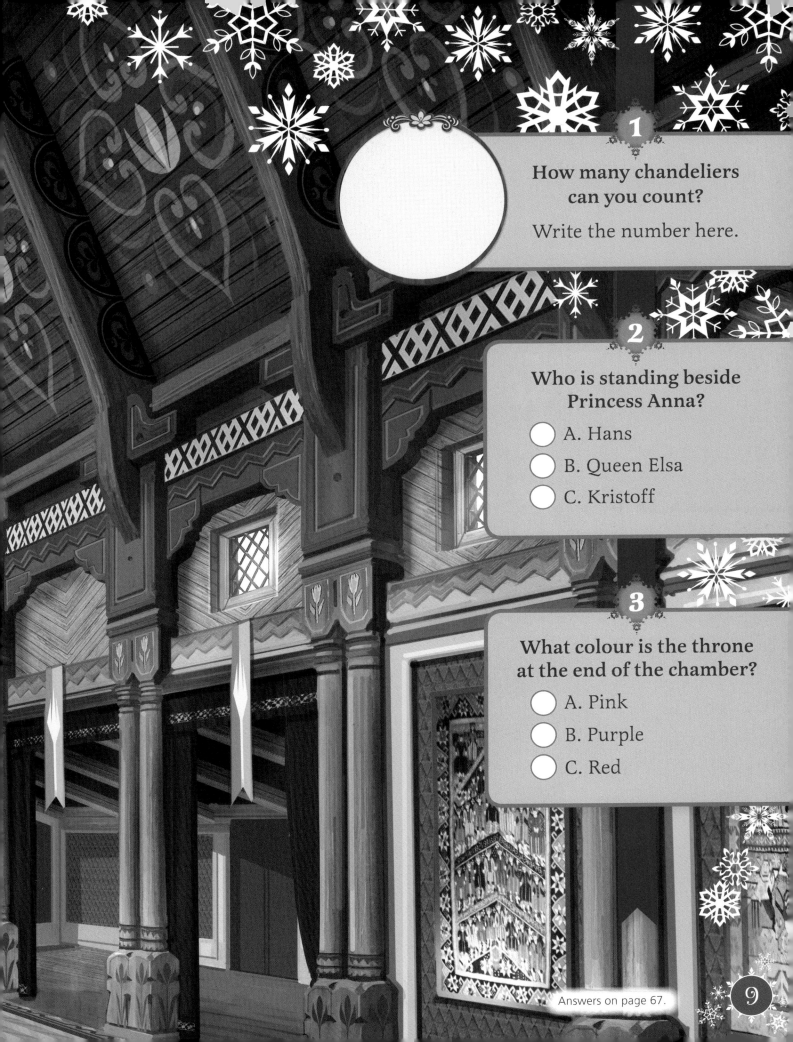

1

How many chandeliers can you count?

Write the number here.

2

Who is standing beside Princess Anna?

○ A. Hans

○ B. Queen Elsa

○ C. Kristoff

3

What colour is the throne at the end of the chamber?

○ A. Pink

○ B. Purple

○ C. Red

Answers on page 67.

Meet Princess Anna

Arendelle's second-born royal princess is called Anna. She yearns to be close to her sister Elsa, the only family that she has left. Sometimes Princess Anna feels pushed away by her big sister, but she's determined to do whatever it takes to get close to her again.

fun-loving · kind · always ready for an adventure · daring · brave · loyal

GETTING TO KNOW YOU

Now Princess Anna wants to find out all about you! Write your name at the top of the scroll, then tick the things that make you happy.

....'s

write your name here

Frosty Favourites

When the snow falls I like to ...
throw snowballs ☐   make snow angels ☐
build snowmen ☐

My favourite treat on a chilly day is ...
hot chocolate with marshmallows ☐
pancakes ☐   banana bread ☐

If I visited Arendelle, I would like to go ...
ice skating ☐   to see the Northern Lights ☐
exploring in the castle ☐

My favourite winter animal is ...
a polar bear ☐   a penguin ☐
a reindeer ☐

WELL DONE!

Open Your Eyes

Anna has a snowy surprise for Elsa in this story!

Manuscript: Alessandro Ferrari; Layout: Arianna Rea; Cleanup: Federica Salfo; Ink: Michela Frare, Cristina Stella; Colourist: Dario Calabria

HERE! JUST AS YOU ASKED, ANNA!

FSHHH

IT'S PERFECT, ELSA!

THANK YOU, BUT... WHY DID YOU WANT ME TO BUILD AN ICE-TRACK WITH A SNOW PILE AT THE END?

IT'S A SURPRISE!

NOW PLEASE GET IN THE SLED AND CLOSE YOUR EYES!

NO WAY! I KNOW WHAT YOU WANT TO DO!

A SECOND LATER...

OPEN YOUR EYES, SISTER...

I CAN'T BELIEVE I'M DOING THIS!

... AND LET YOUR VOICE GO!

!

AHHHHHH!

AHHHHHH!

THUMPF

YES! YES! YES! LET'S DO IT AGAIN!

I KNEW IT...

The End

Lost in the Snow

Oh no, Anna is lost! Help Kristoff and Sven reach Olaf and then guide them to help Anna.

START

FINISH

12

Answer on page 67.

Dancing Days

Anna and her friends are trying to teach Kristoff how to dance! Look at each set of steps, then decide whose turn it is to go next.

Frozen Flurry

Take a whirl through these super snowy puzzles!
How quickly can you complete them all?

A PERFECT MATCH

They say that no two snowflakes are the same. Let's see! Study this
shower and see if you can spot one matching pair.

CRACKED ICE

Can you find three differences between Kristoff and his reflection?

LOST LETTERS

Put one word in front of the words below to make three new ones.

flake

_ _ _ _

ball

man

OUT IN THE COLD

There's a game going on at the ice palace! Who is playing hide-and-seek?
There are three friends to find.

A New Hairstyle

Manuscript: Alessandro Ferrari; Layout: Elisabetta Melaranci; Cleanup: Arianna Rea, Federica Salfo; Ink: Michela Frare, Cristina Stella; Colourist: Dario Calabria

SO... WHAT DO YOU WANT ME TO DO FOR YOU, OLAF?

I WISH I HAD A NEW **STYLE!** TODAY I FEEL HAPPY AND JOYFUL AND I WANT TO LOOK **DIFFERENT!**

I KNOW WHAT TO DO!

FSHHH

FSHROOM

WHOOPS! I'VE PROBABLY GONE TOO FAR!

I LOVE IT! IT'S **EXACTLY** WHAT I WANTED!

 The End

Queen's Plait

Elsa's hairstyle is perfect for a snow queen.
Follow the steps and you'll look like a royal beauty, too!

You will need:

Comb

Ribbon

1

Comb the length of your hair to one side and separate it into three strands.

2

To plait, pull **A** over **B** and **C** over **A**, as shown.

3

Then pull **B** over **C**, and **A** over **B**. Don't make them too tight.

4

Continue plaiting as shown in steps **2** and **3**. At the end, secure your plait with a ribbon.

Ice Skating

Get busy spotting ten differences between the pictures of the frozen lake.
Colour an ice skate each time you find a difference.
How quickly can you find them all?

Use this snowflake code to spell out Anna's message.

a   b   d   i   l   m   n

o   s   t   u   w   y

Answers on page 67.

D _ _ _ _ _ _

_ _

?

21

Meet Queen Elsa

Arendelle's first-born child has a terrible secret – the merest touch from her fingertips can whip up a storm of ice and snow! When Elsa gets frightened or upset, her powers become hard to control. The lonely queen decides to run away, but magic can't be hidden forever ...

thoughtful shy regal enchanted caring at one with the wind and sky

SWISHES AND SPARKLES

Queen Elsa's cloak glitters with a thousand crystals. Use your colouring pencils and crayons to design a new train for the royal queen.

Snow Joke!

Olaf says it's good to giggle every day! Read some of his best funnies, then try them out on your friends.

What did Princess Anna say to Olaf?

You're cool!

What do you call a snowman on rollerskates?

A snow mobile!

What do you call a snowman in the summer?

A puddle!

Where do snowmen do their shopping?

On the Winternet!

How does a snowman travel to work?

By icicle!

What does Olaf eat for breakfast?

Snowflakes!

What do you get if you cross a snowman with a shark?

Frostbite!

A Thousand Words ...

It's time to say it with pictures! Read this *Frozen* story.
When you come to a picture clue, say what you see.
The key below will help you.

Picture Key

 Elsa · Anna · Hans · Marshmallow

On the day of Queen 's coronation, her little sister met a handsome prince called . The prince asked to marry him, but thought this was a bad idea. After fleeing to the North Mountain, used her secret powers to create a magnificent ice palace. Princess and her best friends tried to follow after , but a fierce snowman called drove all of them away.

 The End

Anna's Birthday Surprise

As seen in FROZEN FEVER

It was a special day. The royal castle was holding a surprise party for Princess Anna's birthday!

Queen Elsa used her magical powers to decorate the birthday cake. **Ting!** Two ice figures appeared on the top – Anna and Elsa ice-skating happily side-by-side! Queen Elsa looked at them closely. Everything had to be perfect for the party!

Kristoff hung a banner across the castle courtyard. He had painted 'HAPPY BIRTHDAY ANNA' in rainbow letters.

"Are you sure I can leave you in charge?" asked Elsa.

Kristoff nodded, as she rushed away. It was time for the celebrations to begin!

Elsa tiptoed into Anna's bedroom.

"Wake up, sleepyhead," she smiled. "You've never had a real birthday before, so we're going to make this one extra great!"

The day began with new dresses. There was a skirt decorated with sunflowers for Anna and an emerald gown for the queen.

Elsa held up a string that wound through the castle. Every so often it stopped at a birthday gift. Anna found a bracelet, a cuckoo clock and a bouquet of flowers!

"Achoo!"

Elsa's nose tickled. When she sneezed, white snowmen popped into the air. They tumbled out of sight, then scurried towards the castle courtyard.

"Little brothers!" said Olaf, beaming.

The string wound all over Arendelle. Soon Anna's arms were full of
birthday presents! Elsa began to sneeze more and more. Each time,
a flurry of snowmen appeared. The sisters were so busy following
the string, they didn't notice.

"This day has been amazing," said Anna. "But I think you might need
to go home and rest."

"No, the best is still ahead!"
Elsa insisted, leading her to
Oaken's shop.

Oaken was in the sauna.
When he heard Elsa sneezing,
he brought out a glass bottle.

"How about a medical remedy
of my own invention?" he asked.

Anna nodded gratefully. "I think
we're going to need that."

More snowmen ran into the courtyard – soon they were everywhere! A group began to climb onto Anna's cake. Kristoff grabbed Olaf's head, then tossed it like a bowling ball.

"Incoming!" shouted Olaf, sending the snowmen scattering out of the way.

Over at the clock tower, Anna struggled to carry all of her presents. Queen Elsa started singing a birthday song, even though she felt feverish and weak.

"Please," begged Anna. "You need to rest!"

Suddenly Elsa lost her balance.

"I guess I have a cold," she admitted, as Anna helped her walk back through the castle gates. "I'm sorry I ruined your perfect birthday."

"You didn't ruin anything," said Anna. "Everything was absolutely …"

"SURPRISE!"

Anna and Elsa stood frozen to the spot. In the courtyard were Kristoff, Sven and Olaf, plus a mini-mountain of white snowmen!

Anna blinked at the sight. The birthday banner, balloons and party tables looked amazing. She felt very lucky indeed.

Everybody sang happy birthday. The castle walls echoed with voices, but Kristoff's was the loudest of all. He jumped off the pile of snowmen then held up the cake for Anna to see.

"*Happy birthday, I love you, Anna!*" he chorused, before suddenly catching his breath.

Kristoff's cheeks turned pink. Anna flashed him a happy grin.

A little later, Anna helped Elsa into bed. She needed to rest and sleep off her cold.

"Thank you," whispered Anna. "That was the best birthday present ever."

Elsa thought about all of the gifts that she had chosen.

"Which one?" she wondered out loud.

Anna smiled.

"You finally letting me take care of you," she replied.

The next day, high on the North Mountain, Marshmallow heard a knock on the ice palace doors. Olaf walked in, followed by a parade of tiny snowmen!

At last Kristoff appeared.

"Don't ask," he said with a sigh.

THE END

Guess the Gift

Anna was astonished to open so many birthday gifts!
Read the list below, then see if you can find each word
hiding in the letter grid.

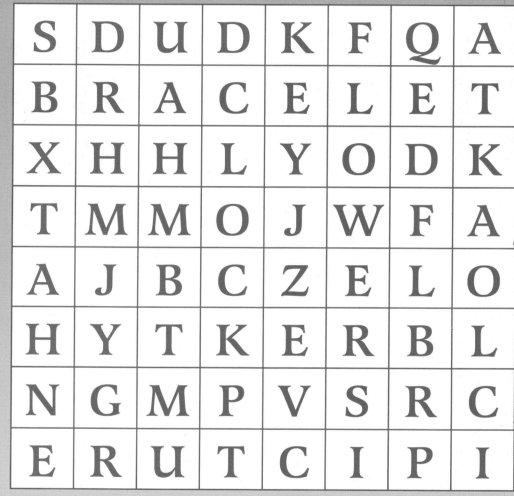

S	D	U	D	K	F	Q	A
B	R	A	C	E	L	E	T
X	H	H	L	Y	O	D	K
T	M	M	O	J	W	F	A
A	J	B	C	Z	E	L	O
H	Y	T	K	E	R	B	L
N	G	M	P	V	S	R	C
E	R	U	T	C	I	P	I

Look carefully. The words could be running
forwards or backwards, up or down.

BRACELET PICTURE

CLOCK FLOWERS

HAT CLOAK

32

Answer on page 68.

Who Ate the Cake?

Who would love to share a slice of Anna's birthday cake?
Look at the pictures, then point to the right one.
The clues below will help you.

1 He is not human.   **2** He does not sing.

3 He has four legs.

Answer on page 68.

33

Counting Snowmen

The royal castle is crammed full of fluffy visitors! Trace over the number of snowmen you can see on this page.

7 10 12

Answer on page 68.

Silly Signs

Olaf is trying to hang up Anna's banner, but his letters have got into a muddle! Four more birthday words have got in a jumble, too. Can you guess what they are?

1 A D C R
C _ _ _ _

2 N A B L O O L
B _ _ _ _ _ _

3 T A R Y P
P _ _ _ _

4 E C A K
C _ _ _

The first letter has been completed for you.

Answers on page 68.

35

From Me to You

What will Elsa think of next? You decide!
Use your crayons and pencils to draw an enchanting
new surprise for Anna's birthday.

Do You Want to Build a Snowman?

Anna adores snow days! Here's her top list of things to do when the world turns white.

1 Wrap up and go on a nature walk. What animal tracks can you spot?

2 Use a stick to carve out a snow maze. Challenge a friend to start in the middle and find their way out.

3 Ask some friends to play tag. Make a rule that you can only step in each other's footprints.

4 Ask a grown-up to help you fill a birdfeeder with seeds. Hang it up outside and wait for some feathery visitors to arrive.

5 Get out your beach buckets and spades, then build an amazing snow castle.

6 Lie down beside your best friend and make snow angels.

Hot or Cold?

Do you know the way to Queen Elsa's magnificent ice palace?
It's hidden out of sight on the lonely North Mountain.

START

FROSTY	COOL	BRIGHT	TOASTY	GLOW
BAKE	WINTER	CHILLY	SNOW	FIRE
SIZZLE	FLAMES	SUNSHINE	ICE	STUFFY
HUMID	TROPICAL	WARM	BLIZZARD	SHIVER
HEAT	GOLDEN	SUMMER	SCORCH	FROZEN

FINISH

Put your finger on the START,
then trace a trail through the
cold and snowy words. Stay
cool and you'll make it all the
way to the palace!

Answer on page 68.

Climb and Slide!

Play a brilliant *Frozen* version of the classic Snakes and Ladders game!

How to play

1 Cut out the counters and choose which character you want to play. Make the spinner by cutting it out and sticking a pencil through the middle. Copy the page if you don't want to cut up your book.

2 Spin the spinner and move forward the number of spaces shown on the side resting on the ground.

3 When you land at the bottom of a yellow swoosh, follow it up. When you land at the top of a trail of footprints, follow them down. The first person to reach the finish wins!

Ask an adult for help!

Never mind. Keep trying!

FINISH 100 99 98
81 82 83
80 79 78
61 62 63
60 59 58
41 42 43
40 39 38

Whooosh!

21 22 23
20 19 18
START 1 2 3

| 97 | 96 | 95 | 94 | 93 | 92 | 91 |

Rrraaa!
Aaahhh!

| 84 | 85 | 86 | 87 | 88 | 89 | 90 |

| 77 | 76 | 75 | 74 | 73 | 72 | 71 |

Follow me!

| 64 | 65 | 66 | 67 | 68 | 69 | 70 |

| 57 | 56 | 55 | 54 | 53 | 52 | 51 |

| 44 | 45 | 46 | 47 | 48 | 49 | 50 |

| 37 | 36 | 35 | 34 | 33 | 32 | 31 |

You'll never make it!

| 24 | 25 | 26 | 27 | 28 | 29 | 30 |

| 17 | 16 | 15 | 14 | 13 | 12 | 11 |

| 4 | 5 | 6 | 7 | 8 | 9 | 10 |

Meet Olaf

When Queen Elsa's magic made a little snowman, Anna gained a new friend. Olaf is a kindly, scatterbrained, bundle of hugs! Although he lives on a cold mountain, he sees the sunny side of everything.

silly

upbeat

hug-loving

cheerful

friendly

CRAZY COLOUR COPY

Would you like a draw a snowman? Carefully copy each square in the box below into the matching empty squares on the right. Hurray, here's Olaf!

WHEN YOU'VE FINISHED, COLOUR IN OLAF'S ORANGE CARROT NOSE!

Snow Troll

Manuscript: Alessandro Ferrari; Layout: Elisabetta Melaranci; Cleanup: Federica Salfo; Ink: Michela Frare; Colourist: Dario Calabria

SOMETHING IS GOING ON IN THE TROLL VALLEY.

WE ARE ALL HERE...

... TO WELCOME A NEW MEMBER OF OUR FAMILY, A TRUE TROLL, GIFTED WITH LOVE, UNDERSTANDING AND MAGIC.

IT'S WITH ENORMOUS PLEASURE THAT I INTRODUCE TO YOU...

... OLAF, THE SNOW TROLL!

I FEEL SO HAPPY MY EYES COULD SNOW!

YEAHHH!

CLAP

CLAP

I SUSPECT TROLLS WILL NEVER BE THE SAME FROM NOW ON...

I WANT TO BE A SNOW TROLL TOO!

POP

The End

Who Are You?

Sisters can be quite different from each other, but still feel a close bond. Do you think you are more like Elsa or Anna? Take this quiz to find out!

1 Your friends would describe you as:
◇ A. Regal.
◇ B. Bold.

2 When you meet someone new, you are:
◇ A. Warm but reserved.
◇ B. Excited and chatty.

3 Your favourite season is:
◇ A. Winter - you don't mind the cold at all.
◇ B. Spring - you like sunshine and flowers.

4 When you're with friends, you are:
◇ A. The responsible one who wants everyone to do what's right.
◇ B. The one who's always coming up with creative ideas and fun things to do.

5 Others admire your:
◇ A. Leadership skills.
◇ B. Persistence and optimism.

A's
Elsa

You're reserved and cautious, and sometimes a little stubborn, but you're loving and protective of your family. You're a natural leader who always wants to do the right thing.

B's
Anna

You enjoy meeting people and have an optimistic can-do attitude. You have a romantic nature and enjoy adventure and new experiences, but you're not just a dreamer - you never give up on your goals.

Dazzle and Shine

Let's shine a light on this page!
Draw a line to match each shadow to the right owner.

1 Anna

2 Olaf

3 Kristoff

A

B

C

D

One shadow doesn't have a match. Can you guess who it belongs to?

Answers on page 68.

Marsh-Memories

Marshmallow has put up a picture to remind him of his friends in Arendelle. Take a look, then hide it under a piece of paper. Now try and answer the quiz questions below.

1 Who is standing at the front of the picture?

2 What colour is Anna's cape?

3 What is Sven standing next to?

Answers on page 68.

Name Game

Imagine that you are a special visitor coming to Arendelle.
What would your royal name be? Pick the word that you like best
from each frame, then put them together to make a magical new title!

1
Lady
Prince
Princess
Excellency
Duke

2
Otto
Natasha
Elizabetta
Crystal
Felix

3
Winter
Blizzard
Emerald
Starshine
Shard

4
Frost
Diamond
Sleigh-belle
Ice-dome
Glacier

Magic in the Mountains

Elsa's magic is powerful. Join up the dots to finish this enchanting portrait of the ice queen.

Now colour Elsa in!

13
12
11
10
9
8
7
6
5
4
3
2
1

Cute Card!

Make this card for a friend who loves *Frozen*! There's a cute pop-up surprise inside.

You will need:
A4 card
pencil
ruler
scissors
glue
glitter
felt-tips

Cut out the pictures on this page and use them to create your card or copy the page if you don't want to cut up your book.

© Disney

1 Fold a piece of A4 paper neatly in half to make a card shape. Use a ruler to draw two 3cm lines (about 3cm apart) in the centre of the crease. Cut along these lines.

2 Open the paper and push the snipped section in, so that when you fold the card again, it folds inside.

3 Next, fold a piece of A4 card in half and glue the paper inside.

4 Colour and cut out the pictures on the opposite page and use them to decorate the front of your card.

5 Cut out Anna and Elsa and glue them to the inside pop-up section of your card. Write your message inside and give it to a friend!

Ask an adult for help!

Meet Kristoff

He might be a bit rough around the edges, but Kristoff's got a heart of gold. The outdoorsman earns a living harvesting ice and selling it to the people of Arendelle. Kristoff is happiest when he's up in the lonely mountains, working alongside his beloved reindeer, Sven.

tough noble warm-hearted honest determined to do what's right

ICE HARVESTERS

Ice harvesters like to sing while they work! Kristoff has been cutting blocks into lots of different shapes. Colour the matching shapes in the square below to reveal the ice sculpture that he's made.

Answer on page 68.

The King of Hugs

IN THE TROLL VALLEY, OLAF CAN'T BELIEVE HIS EARS...

I'M THE **HAPPIEST** SNOWMAN!

... GRAND PABBIE HAS JUST ANNOUNCED HIS ANNUAL CONTEST.

THE PRIZE THIS YEAR? EACH TROLL WILL **HUG THE WINNER** TWICE A DAY FOR AN **ENTIRE** YEAR!

OLAF HOPES TO WIN!

THE WINNER WILL BE THE MOST HUGGED PERSON EVER!

IT SOUNDS LIKE A FULL TIME JOB TO ME.

THE JOB OF MY LIFE...

TO WIN THE CONTEST, YOU MUST SING THE LOUDEST...

Manuscript: Alessandro Ferrari; Layout: Elisabetta Melaranci; Cleanup: Arianna Rea, Federica Salfo; Ink: Michela Frare, Cristina Stella; Colourist: Dario Calabria

"... USING THE BIGGEST HORN YOU CAN FIND!"

I'LL CARVE MINE OUT OF **WOOD**!

I FOUND MINE IN A **CAVE**!

WE ARE **MAKING** OURS!

OH NO... I DON'T HAVE A HORN! WHAT CAN I DO?

WE'LL FIGURE IT OUT TOGETHER, OLAF. WE'LL HELP YOU!

WE?

OF COURSE WE!

SOON IT'S CONTEST DAY!

ALL THE TROLLS ARE REALLY LOUD...

... SOME OF THEM ARE EXTRAORDINARILY LOUD!

WITH THE HELP OF HIS FRIENDS...

SING AS **LOUDLY** AS YOU CAN, OLAF! WE BELIEVE IN YOU!

THANK YOU, THANK YOU, THANK YOU!

... OLAF GETS READY TO BEAT THEM ALL WITH HIS ICE HORN!

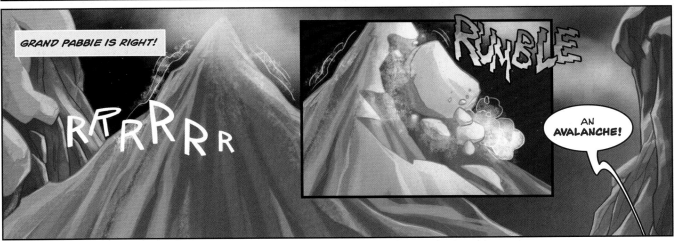

Whooooooosh!

PHEEEEW! THAT WAS CLOSE.

LUCKILY WE'RE ALL SAFE!

?!

OLAF? YOU'RE RIGHT, SVEN! OLAF IS MISSING!

OLAF! WHERE ARE YOU?

HE SHOULD BE THERE SOMEWHERE...

ARE WE REALLY LOOKING FOR A **SNOWMAN** IN THE **SNOW**?

!

SNIFF SNIFF

!

SVEN? WHAT HAPPENED?

OLAF! YOU'RE SAFE!

WOW! I THINK I WON THE CONTEST!

LOOKS LIKE YOU'RE GETTING A YEAR FULL OF HUGS, OLAF! THAT MAKES YOU THE **KING OF HUGS!**

HOORAY!

The End

Secret Place

Olaf and his friends need to reach Grand Pabbie. Guide them down the right path!

START

FINISH

Answer on page 68.

She Said, She Said

How well do you know Anna and Elsa? Use a
blue crayon or pencil to colour in the snowflakes next to
Elsa's sayings. Colour Anna's sayings in purple.

"That's no blizzard, that's my sister."

"I don't dance. But my sister does."

"I never knew winter could be so beautiful."

"I want to help!"

Answers on page 68.

Meet Sven

Sven doesn't just pull Kristoff's sleigh – he's also his best friend. The loyal pair have been a team ever since they can remember. Sven doesn't say too much, but it only takes a few noisy reindeer snorts to work out what's on his mind!

fearless

true

faithful

willing

strong

SILLY SLEIGHS

Whoa, there! Sven and Kristoff need your help! Can you find the missing jigsaw piece to fill each gap in the picture? Draw a line to match each shape to its space in the scene.

Colour me Pretty!

Anna and Elsa love whirling and twirling around the castle ballroom!
Use your favourite pens and crayons to colour the sisters in.

Family Forever

Cut along here.

Answers

Pages 8-9
Step into Arendelle
1. 2
2. A
3. C

Page 14
Lost in the Snow

Page 15
Dancing Days

A.

B.

C.

Pages 16-17
Frozen Flurry
A Perfect Match

Cracked Ice

Lost Letters
snow

Out in the Cold

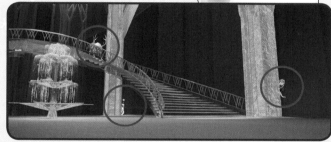

Pages 20-21
Ice Skating

Anna's message:
Do you want to build
a snowman?

Answers

Page 32
Guess the Gift

S	D	U	D	K	F	Q	A
B	R	A	C	E	L	E	T
X	H	H	L	Y	O	D	K
T	M	M	O	J	W	F	A
A	J	B	C	Z	E	L	O
H	Y	T	K	E	R	B	L
N	G	M	P	V	S	R	C
E	R	U	T	C	I	P	I

Page 33
Who Ate the Cake?
Sven would love a slice of birthday cake.

Page 34
Counting Snowmen
10

Page 35
Silly Signs
1. CARD
2. BALLOON
3. PARTY
4. CAKE

Page 39
Hot or Cold?

FROSTY · COOL · BRIGHT · TOASTY · GLOW
BAKE · WINTER · CHILLY · SNOW · FIRE
SIZZLE · FLAMES · SUNSHINE · ICE · STUFFY
HUMID · TROPICAL · WARM · BLIZZARD · SHIVER
HEAT · GOLDEN · SUMMER · SCORCH · FROZEN

Page 46
Dazzle and Shine
1. D   2. B
3. C
Shadow 'A' belongs to Elsa.

Page 47
Marsh-Memories
1. Elsa
2. pink
3. The fountain

Page 53
Ice Harvesters
Kristoff has made a heart.

Page 60
Secret Place

Page 61
She Said, She Said
Anna:
"That's no blizzard, that's my sister."
"I never knew winter could be so beautiful."
"I want to help!"
Elsa:
"I don't dance. But my sister does."

Page 63
Silly Sleighs